His Curvy Housemaid

by
Euryia Larsen

Description

Max Harrison

My mother has decided that I work too much. Such an innocent statement when in truth she had me kidnapped by the very men I hired to protect her. So now I'm on a forced vacation at the Hillview Resorts. I know this vacation is going to be a nightmare until I walk out of the bathroom to find a beautiful young woman making my bed.

Emmy Jackson

In the year since we lost our father, my life has been one problem after another. My mother doesn't leave her room but someone has to take care of my little brother and sister. So I put on my big girl pants and get to work. Then the gorgeous Mr. Harrison walks out of the bathroom in the buff.

How am I supposed to solve this situation without losing my job? He says he wants to take care of us but can I believe him? Can I believe him even after his girlfriend shows up?

Chapter 1

Max

"Mr. Harrison, your mother is on line one. She's insisting on speaking with you otherwise she says she will come to your office and make a scene," my assistant informs me.

I groan to myself in frustration. As Martha Harrison's youngest child, my mother was fond of making my life difficult. My older brother and sister were married and had children so she had turned her attention to me. At thirty-four, I was happier running my cyber security business and not getting involved with any woman long-term. This frustrated my mother to no end.

"Hello, Mom. I have a meeting shortly so I can't talk long."

"You can never talk long, Max. I saw that you were spotted with that woman again. You know how I feel about Carmella Dannings. If the dictionary had an image for 'gold-digging tramp' it would be of her face. Do you realize she was seen having lunch with Ken Mackie? Although, it was pretty obvious food wasn't on her mind," my mother ranted at me.

With a loud sigh, I told her, "Carmella is nothing to me but a way to deal with my baser desires." I didn't feel like telling her right then that I'd already ended things with Carmella. I'd discovered she was trying to discover company secrets to sell them to the highest bidder, like Ken Mackie. Unfortunately, it also turned out she was batshit crazy, again something I didn't feel like going into with my mom.

"I swear you're a carbon copy of your father before he met me, Maxwell. Will you please join me for dinner tonight? I miss my son."

I hung my head in resignation. "Fine, what time and where?"

"Are you all finished with your meetings by seven?"

"Seven will work. Where do you want to meet?"

"Oh, I found the cutest place. I'll send Chris to pick you up. It'll be easier that way."

"Fine. It has been too long, Mom. I'm sorry about that."

"I know, Max. I just worry about you like I worry about all of my children. Since I lost your father, I've realized how short life is. It goes by in the blink of an eye." I hear her pause and I know she's wiping her eyes. My dad died of a heart attack two years ago and she will always miss the man she loved with her whole heart.

"I promise I'll do better. I'm going to finish my meetings and I'll see you tonight. Okay?"

"I'm so glad. Thank you, Max. I love you."

"I love you, too, Mom." As I hang up the phone I sigh, my heart heavy with the guilt I feel. I've shouldn't have been avoiding my Mother. It wasn't right.

With a shake of my head to clear my thoughts. I go back to work and start to prepare for the meetings to make them as quick as possible without being rushed. I'd make sure and gave my mom undivided attention at dinner.

With a yawn, I realized I must have fallen asleep in the car on the way to dinner. Quickly looking at my watch, I frown as I realize it's after nine. Rolling down the privacy winder I ask, "Chris, where are we? We should have arrived at dinner by now? What is going on?"

Before he could answer me, my phone rang and I narrowed my eyes as I saw it was my mother. "What's going on, Mom?"

"Don't be mad, Maxwell. You never listen to me and I've been really worried about you. You always seem so tired lately. After your Dad's heart attack I had to do something to prevent the same thing from happening to my baby."

"Mom, I just had a check up and my heart is just fine."

"And yet I'd bet all of our money that he told you to lower your stress and stop working so hard."

"Maybe," I muttered, not wanting to admit she was right.

I couldn't stop the smile that formed at hearing her musical giggle. "Then maybe you won't be too mad at me. Chris is taking you to a wonderful new resort so that you can take a week off. I've already taken care of setting everything up for you at work. Your assistant has postponed all of your meetings until next week. She will only contact you if it is a real emergency. Turns out she was just as worried about you as I was."

I sighed heavily as I listened to her. Rubbing my fingers across my forehead I asked, "And what am I supposed to do at this resort for a week?"

"Whatever you want as long as it's not work related. Read a good book. Hike, explore nature, swim, whatever. Please do this for me, Max. I swear on all that is holy I will never do this again." I could hear the true worry in her voice and I knew that ever since Dad's heart attack she feared losing her children the same way.

"Never again, Mom. I mean it." I tried to interject a level of sternness into my voice. "Fine, I'll spend a week here in deference to you and my doctor."

Waking up the next morning without an alarm blaring was a luxury I'd forgotten about. I'd slept harder than I'd in a very long time. I woke up ache free, feeling content. It was a foreign feeling and one that I really liked.

I walked around the suite drinking a cup of coffee and checking out my surroundings. The suite Mom booked for me was admittedly very nice. Every window had phenomenal views. I was determined to make the best of this week. At the very least, Carmella wouldn't know where I was.

After looking at the brochures about the nearby town and hiking trails, I found myself looking forward to checking out a few of the shops in town. Maybe I would even go for a an actual jog that went somewhere instead of on a treadmill. Going into the bathroom, I took a shower to start the day off.

Chapter 2

Max

I saw her silhouette first, swaying to music with curves Marilyn Monroe would envy, as I entered the bedroom after taking shower. When she stepped into the light, my jaw dropped. I was greeted with the soft scent of orange blossom, something I didn't expect with her cleaning products in the basket next to her. The scent was barely there too, just a hint, nothing overpowering.

Like I was an inexperienced teenager, I instantly started to harden. Shock rippled though me. No woman had ever managed to get my dick to move just by looking at her. But this goddess had my cock pulsing with blood and my body aching the second I lay eyes on her. Her presence shook me down to my core.

"Oh!" she squeaked when she turned around and saw me just standing there staring like the idiot I was. "I-I'm so sorry. I didn't hear anyone when I called out. My name is Emmy," she said, her cheeks pink. Picking up her basket of supplies she added, "I'm so sorry, I'll come back later and finish cleaning."

Before she could take a step I quickly told her, "I'm Max, Max Harrison."

"I know who you are," she said with a small smile. I was entranced with her beautiful eyes. They were brilliant and green like sparkling emeralds, the perfect topping to her unbelievable body. Instantly, I started picturing her stripping down in front of me, what she'd look like naked.

I couldn't let her leave yet. "Emmy, I'm finished in the bathroom if you want to work in there. I'll quickly get dressed in the closet. There's no need to come back."

"If you're sure. I don't want to intrude. We're supposed to work in the background, not to be seen and definitely not to bother the guests." Her voice was sweet and made me wonder what she'd sound like gasping my name while I filled her with my cock as I claimed her as mine.

It actually took me a second to respond, as I was too caught up in her beauty to think. Her hair was a warm chestnut and sparkled under the ceiling lights, and her lush pouty lips had my mouth watering, feeling almost desperate to taste her. Her hotel uniform was loose and obviously designed to hide her curves, but it was completely failing in that regard.

"Mr. Harrison?" she asked, shaking me from my daydream.

"Yes, sorry," I replied. "I'm sure."

Emmy nodded and walked into the bathroom. I quickly got myself dressed in jeans and a tshirt before walking to the window table and sat down. Once seated I opened my laptop to make it appear like I wasn't one of those creepy guys hoping to pull the maid into bed. Well, I was but I wanted forever, not just today.

My mind wandered over everything I was dying to know about my little siren. Did she have a man? The thought angered me and my hands tightened in a fist. Taking deep breaths to calm myself down I forced a smile to my face as walked to her cart by the door, carrying out the used towels with her.

"So, Emmy, why housekeeping?"

She smiled at my question for several long minutes before she finally replied, "We lost my father last year and my mom has taken it extremely hard. He didn't leave a lot in the way of life insurance, so as the oldest I needed to help. So I quit college, move back home, and got a job here. The pays not great but it covers what we need and it allows me to meet my little brother and sister at their school bus."

"Those are very good reasons but it's a shame you had to give up going to college."

"I'll go back at some point. Family is too important at the moment."

I smiled at her response. Too often I came across young professionals that lacked all drive. Emmy took her responsibility seriously. "So what about your personal life?" I asked. "Married? Kids?"

Emmy gave me a strange look, one I wasn't sure how to read. "I'm single," she replied.

'Not for long.' I instantly thought.

"Mr. Harrison, would you like me to change the sheets?" My beauty asked.

"No need. That seems like a waste of resources to wash barely slept in sheets."

With a nod, Emmy started to make the bed. I watched her swift sure movements, trying to make it appear that I was working on my computer. "How long will you be staying with us, Mr. Harrison?"

"Call me Max, please," I told her. "Mr. Harrison was my father." I loved the pretty blush that turned her pinks a shade that reminded me of cotton candy.

"A week. Longer if my mother has her way. This a forced vacation because she's convinced I work too much," I chuckled.

"Don't stay cooped up in your room then. The weather is beautiful and there are so many things to do both near the hotel and those that you'd want to drive to."

"My mother would love you, Emmy," I answered with a chuckle as I stood up and gathered up my trash to make it easier for her.

"Would she?"

"Oh most definitely."

"Maybe next time she can come to visit as well." The bed was made, looking better than when I arrived. Emmy walked up and put her hand on the trash container to take it from me.

I knew that once she empty she'd be gone and I didn't want her to leave yet. I was enjoying her company too much. Without even realizing it, I leaned closer to her, close enough to smell her sweetness and feel the heat from her body. It took every ounce of my strength to not pull her into my arms.

I wondered if she could see the bulge in my pants so she would know what she was doing to me. She seemed just as lost in my eyes as I was hers and actually leaned in closer. Licking her bottom lip, her gaze quickly moved from my eyes to my lips and back.

"I want you," I told her.

Her eyes widened at the words I hadn't meant to say outloud. "You...you want me?" she whispered. "For your housekeeper or for...something else?"

"To join me for dinner this evening." I her as I leaned in and kissed her. When our lips met, I almost lost control. My hands found her hips, and as I was about to pull her closer to me, she actually leaned in and pressed her body against mine.

I felt her breasts against my chest. They were big, soft but firm at the same time. They were perfect like the rest of her. I knew that this girl was mine. She had to be. I couldn't let her slip away from me. But just as I began to pull her closer, she broke our embrace and leapt back and put a hand over her lips like I'd shocked her. "I-I'm sorry," she said quickly. "That was very inappropriate of me."

"Don't be silly, Emmy."

"No, I-I should go," she stammered. And before I could protest again, she snatched the door open and rushed out of the room.

I sighed heavily as I realized I hadn't even gotten her phone number. Emmy had come crashing into my life like a meteor and left just as quickly. I wasn't about to let that be the end of things, though. I was Max Harrison and I didn't get to where I was by not going after the things that I wanted, and now I wanted Emmy, and she was going to be mine.

Chapter 3

Emmy

In the year since we lost our father, my life has been one problem after another. Mom rarely leaves her room even with the anti-depressants she takes. Unfortunately the world doesn't want to stop even if you want it to. I just turned twenty-one but knew after my father's funeral I couldn't return to college. Someone had to take care of my younger brother and sister. Someone had to pay the bills. With no one else to turn to, it fell to me.

After figuring out Papa's life insurance and talking with a legal aide friend of mine, I realized the financial situation was quickly going to become dire. I made sure to talk to Marc and Anna's school about the situation. They made a note to keep me informed of any issues. Marc had some anger issues but Anna seemed to be doing well.

I was fortunate to get a job as a waitress working the hours the kids were in school. That is until I had to leave one too many times to head to the school about Marc fighting. Then a pipe burst in the kitchen during a cold snap that wiped out most of the money I'd managed to keep in the bank.

I applied for aide from the state but was denied because of my age. They felt I was too young to require food stamps. Especially since I didn't have legal custody of Marc and Anna. Just when I was starting to lose hope, I was able to get a job in Housecleaning. It was a surprise that they hired because during the interview, I received an emergency call about Anna. She's broken her arm falling out of a tree.

As I got my footing at the new job, I'd been scrambling for the last two months trying to make ends meet. My bank account, like my fuel gauge in my car, were all but empty. One of the rooms I had to clean left a $20 tip which would pay for gas until payday.

Now, I was trying desperately not to freak out. I was supposed to be responsible, working and taking care of my family should have been the only things I kept focus on. So what had I ended up doing? Kissing Max Harrison… "What were you thinking, Emmy?" I groaned, convinced he was going to complain and I would lose my job.

I don't know what made me angrier at myself, the fact that I'd kissed him or the fact that I knew why I'd done it. I was struggling with everything and I felt this desperate need to be young and carefree again. I wanted to be back in college, learning and having fun being young and free.

That wasn't my reality anymore, no matter how much I missed it. When Max Harrison had come out of his bathroom in the buff, it threw me completely off balance. He was hot with a capitol H. He was the kind of gorgeous that would get him tons of girls without being absurdly rich like he was. He was clearly older than I was, which made it even hotter, a killer jaw and a head of model-esque slicked back dark brown hair, and he had a physique that belonged on a magazine cover.

My body had started responding the minute I'd seen him. Seeing *everything* had caused me to make the most embarrassing sound before I could leave the room. I'd done a good job at not letting on I hoped, but obviously had given something away if he'd moved in on me like that. Maybe he was the type of guy who though he was God's gift to women and seeing everything meant I wanted everything.

Somehow I didn't think that was even close to being correct. He'd said he wanted me to join him for dinner. That didn't really scream torrid affair. He hadn't grabbed me by the wrist and pulled me back into the room, he'd instead let me run. Taking a deep calming breath, I tried to stop berating myself. There's no doubt in my mind that I would have let him bend me over that bed and fuck my brains out.

"Shit," I grumbled as I pushed my cart into it's parking slot in housekeeping. This was a really crappy situation, and I could only hope beyond hope that he wouldn't lodge a complaint. He was gorgeous and I admittedly wanted him. In my life right now, though, I would have to make sure to put my priorities before everything else.

I walked into the manager's office. I really like Carolyn she was fair and really tried to work with my schedule requirements. "Hey Carolyn, I have a few items for lost and found. Most charge cords and the like. Mr. 207 left behind expensive sunglasses and $1500 in cash underneath it. It didn't look like a tip because he left a $20 by the housekeeping sign."

"Thank you for being honest as always, Emmy. Make sure you log everything and if 207 doesn't claim any of it including the cash, it'll be yours in a week. How are things at home? Things any better with the kiddos?"

"Anna gets her cast off in two weeks. Marc is trying. I spend time with each of them every evening just talking to them about anything and everything. It seems to be helping. Mom is the same." I looked up at Carolyn from the Lost and Found Log Book and smiled at her sadly.

Carolyn smiled at me like a proud momma and I had to fight back the burning in my eyes. "I'm sure she appreciates everything even if she doesn't acknowledge it. I'm proud of the woman you are. The responsibility you've taken over most established adults wouldn't do."

"Thank you, that really means a lot. It's hard but how can I do anything but be there. I love them."

"That much is obvious. Oh! I almost forgot. The VIP Room. Mr. Harrison. He called down and asked if you could return to the room before you left for the day. He wanted to make sure you got your tip since you're off tomorrow."

I sat there and blinked at her in surprise. "My tip?"

"That's what he said. He had nothing but good things to say how you indulged his incessant questions while taking care of the room. He made sure to tell me that when you realized he was in the room, you offered to come back but he insisted you stay. He said he wasn't sure how to spend his days but you gave him some really good ideas," Carolyn gushed.

"He did?"

"He did. Thank you for making him happy. Max Harrison is a notorious guest. He was far from happy when he checked in," she smiled as she explained.

"Carolyn... um, I need to be honest, he kissed me before I left. I know it's against the rules but I really hope you don't fire me."

"Emmy you're a a gorgeous girl of course he'd be interested. As for the rules. They only say you aren't allowed to seduce guests. If he wants to ask you out I say go for it. He's gorgeous. I promise I'm fully aware of the situation and even if one of the employees says something, you'll be fine. I promise."

I looked at her in surprise before I sighed and nodded my head. If Max really wanted to give me a tip, I couldn't certainly use it. "Alright, thank you. I'll stop by his room after take care of my cart. Thanks again, Carolyn, for everything."

"Oh shush you, go on." I smiled as she shoo'd me away with her hands before returning back to the paperwork on her desk.

Chapter 4

Max

I couldn't get that brief kiss with Emmy off my mind. The combination of her beauty and confidence had my balls tight and my body on fire for her. This wasn't some dumb club bimbo who'd say whatever she thought I wanted to hear just so she could try and get some money out of me. This was a girl who worked hard for her family, the kind of girl who could be a real match for me.

All of a sudden, my future was clear to me. Now I just had to convince her to give me a chance, to give us a chance. I would take care of her family as if they were my own. I knew my mom would love Emmy and maybe, just maybe, she could help Emmy's mom.

I smiled as I heard a soft knock on the door. Opening it with a smile, I said, "Emmy! I'm so glad you came back. I wanted to provide your tip in person so that no one else will get it by accident."

"I appreciate that Mr. Harrison but I'm off for the next two days so I won't be your housemaid."

"Carolyn told me. To be honest, Emmy. I was afraid you wouldn't come back after I took liberties and kissed you while you were just trying to work. I meant what I said, I really want to take you to dinner and get to know you."

She looked at me skeptically and I could see the debate in warring in her eyes. "Fine, you're in luck. My brother and sister are spending the night with friends so I'm available to go to dinner with you."

With a wide grin, I pulled her into my arms and kissed her deeply. After several long minutes, Emmy finally pushed back from me panting. "Dinner."

With a chuckle, I took her hand in mine and pulled her out of the room. "Dinner it is then."

Emmy

Dinner was wonderful and the company was even better. I found myself telling Max about the Chaos of the last year. More than once he commented how I had him now and that I was going to let him help us. I wasn't sure I really believed that at first but as the evening progressed and learned so much about each other, I found myself hoping.

I was walking him back to his suite, when he suddenly pulled me into his arms. Max groaned into the kiss and pressed me back, more powerful than I'd expected. Together, we crashed into the wall, rattling the pictures on the wall. He didn't care. His lips crushed mine, his tongue making love to my mouth, and I never wanted him to stop.

Pressing my body into his, I moaned softly as I writhed against him. He groaned to match. I'd wanted Max since I first saw him. Resisting him was as impossible as expecting sun to not rise or set in a day. When his lips moved to my neck, I leaned my head back. The hand in my hair tightened, holding me there, and he paused.

With his mouth hovering just above my skin, he held me trapped, and I made no move to resist. Lightly, the tip of his tongue tickled the tendon. Then he kissed. That became a nip. My pulse thrummed in the pit of my stomach, and I could feel the moisture between my legs, but he was taunting me, proving I couldn't do a damned thing to stop him. I didn't want to. "Please," I begged forgetting we were still in the hotel hallway.

"Not here," he said, pulling himself from my grasp. Before I could reply, he slid an arm beneath me, lifting me all too easily. "Just don't let me hurt you," he whispered.

"You won't."

He made it to his suite quickly, carrying me as if I weighed nothing. Walking down a hall to bedroom, he pushed it open with his back. Gently, he laid me on the bed and followed me down. I opened my knees to make room for the width of his hips, welcoming his body against mine. One of his strong arms held his weight off me. "God, I want you," he breathed, then kissed me.

That was exactly what I wanted to hear. Gripping the back of his head, I held him close, showing him what I wanted. My legs pressed against his thighs, locking him between my knees. His hand traveled down my body, tracing along my ribs to my hip, making me feel so small and delicate beneath him. Sexy. Desirable. Even wanton.

So many times, I'd felt like I was just the easiest option, but that wasn't the case with Max. He touched me like he wanted nothing else. His mouth moved down my throat, tasting my skin, kissing every inch of my neck with a desire I'd never felt from a man. I surrendered to it, arching my body into him, grasping at his broad shoulders through the soft shirt to hold him closer

I needed more, wanted everything. Max turned me on like no other man. I had to kiss his chest, to touch it. Yanking the hem of his shirt free of his pants, my hands slid beneath, feeling the skin at his waist. Slowly, I let them roam. Men like him were what women dreamed of. I'd never expected it to happen, though. I never honestly believed Max would actually feel the same way about me.

My palms caressed the ridges of his abs and kept moving higher, making him suck in a breath. Then down, exploring the feel of him, trying to identify the imperfections I couldn't see in the dimly lit room. He was amazing.

My mouth teased one nipple through the cloth of his shirt, then kissed the flat muscle above it as I sought his mouth. He met me halfway with a growl deep in the back of his throat. Damn, this man could kiss, but I wanted more. Sucking at his lips, tangling my tongue with his, I let my hands find their way down until my fingers tripped over the waistband of his jeans. That was what I wanted. I fumbled at the buckle of his belt, hoping to sneak inside.

He chuckled, breaking our kiss. "If you do that, I won't stop."

My answer was breathy. "I don't want you to stop."

He pressed his hips into me, rock hard through the fabric – and it felt so damned good. His mouth sucked at my neck as his hand slid under my back. Then he shifted, rolling over, pulling me above him. With me trapped on his lap, he sat up, but his hands were still moving. Taking his time about it, he guided my shirt higher, giving me every chance to stop him.

I grabbed the hem and wrenched the fabric over my head, tossing it out of reach. As the shirt fell away, he paused. I could see dim reflections in his dark eyes as he slid first one bra strap from my shoulder, then the other, drinking in everything as I reached back to release the clasp. The material dropped into my lap.

Max sighed softly, the same sound people make when viewing a great work of art. It wasn't one I was used to hearing in the bedroom. Gently, tenderly, his strong hands moved to my ribs, meeting the swell of my breasts, his thumbs trailing higher. Slowly, the pads drifted across my nipples, making the flesh tighten almost painfully. Then he did it again, the feeling so exquisite. "Max," I whimpered.

"You have me, baby," Max promised, his hands worshiping my body. Again he rolled, tossing me onto my back, sliding the last of my clothing down over my hips before he reached for his own. His mouth kissed a line from my jaw to my navel as he eased back. The sound of fabric rustling on skin filled the room when he tugged his arms free of his shirt.

His touch was like fire, sparks igniting beneath his mouth. His eyes were filled with a need so intense I couldn't describe it. I lay there, panting, afraid he was going to stop, and watched his hands slowly work the button of his pants.

He raked his eyes across my naked body and bent his mouth to my ankle. His pants made a soft thud when they met the floor, but his mouth didn't stop. It moved along the outside of my leg, over my hip as he crept closer, up my ribs, until his tongue found one nipple, his hand the other.

I arched into it, moaning, hoping he wouldn't stop, feeling his lean, hard hips against my thighs. "Max," I pleaded. Releasing my breast, he moved to my mouth. His lips found mine for only a quick caress, then he paused. I could feel him right there, pressing into my cleft. I shifted, sliding my dampness against him.

He groaned loudly as he tilted his hips, prodding me, slowly pushing in. I sucked in a breath and tried to impale myself, but the man caught my waist in his hand. Holding me there, he took his time, teasing me with every inch until I was mewling for more. Then he thrust. For all I knew, I was surrendering my soul, but I didn't care. He felt so damned good, filling me as his rock-hard body pinned me to the mattress.

Every dream I had were of this, the man of my dreams wanting me as badly as I wanted him. Max held me, slowly withdrawing just to slide a little deeper. He kissed me, his tongue demanding my complete attention, and slid into me again, over and over, driving my body higher, teasing every nerve in my core. I clung to him, nails gouging his back, my voice tinting each gasp of air, thinking of nothing but the swell of pleasure building inside, wanting to have all of him.

"You feel so good," he whispered into my ear. "So damned good." His voice was pure seduction, demanding that I surrender to it and I succumbed. I was finally with him, and our slick bodies ground together in perfect harmony. A cry of desire escaped my lips, smothered with his mouth, and his hips drove me to places I'd never experienced. Slowly, deeply, tenderly, Max caressed every sensation from me that my body could handle, filling me with pleasures I hadn't even known were possible.

Worries about my family, about finances, about everything vanished as my body worshiped him, every nerve completely under his control. Over and over he thrust, and I took it all, delicate skin stretched taut with the size of him, sensitive nipples wonderfully tormented as they brushed against his chest. Each stroke sent flames along my nerves, burning away my restraint, quenched only by the sweat on our skin, until, with a throaty gasp, my body found release. I came, clenched hard against him.

My eyes pressed closed to focus on the waves of pleasure running through me as he grunted in the back of his throat. A few more strokes rode me to the end, then he shuddered as he came. When he tensed, our eyes met, holding each other for that one moment, just long enough to make this feel real, like it meant something before he relaxed. His head dropped to my shoulder, his elbows holding his mass off me while we both sucked back long gasps of air.

Languidly running my fingers down the mass of hair laying against his neck, I savored the moment, feeling so complete lying in the arms of my man. The last flutters of my orgasm passed as I caught my breath, but I just wanted to hold him, to be close like this for one second longer. It took a while before he shifted, kissing me as he withdrew. Then he moved to lie beside me on the bed.

Max took a long breath, chuckling in the middle. "That was not quite what I had planned for tonight."

"Oh?" I rolled onto my side to look at him. "And what was my big man supposed to be doing?"

"Yours?" He scooted closer, reaching up to palm the back of my head. I nodded under his hand.

"I think this means you're officially my boyfriend unless you disagree?"

"Mm. I do like the part where we can do this again. The boyfriend part sounds interesting, too." His smile sparkled in the dim light. "And I can only guess that if I refuse, I won't be allowed to do that again, huh?"

"Exactly."

"Well, you drive a hard bargain, but it seems you have a deal, baby." He caught my wrist. "Emmy? Did I hurt you?"

"Do I act like I'm hurt?"

"No, but..." He lifted my hand to his lips and kissed my knuckles. "You're so much smaller than me and I don't ever want to hurt you."

With a smile, I sat up. "You were gentle. Trust me. I can take a whole lot more than that."

Another flicker of that smile appeared. "Yeah?"

"Oh yeah."

He released my hand and caught my hip, pulling me against him. Lying side by side on the soft mattress, he just looked at me, drinking in the moment. I didn't mind. It made me feel like I might matter for more than just right now. "Help me get this right?" he asked.

"Get what right?"

"Us." His eyes flicked between mine. "You're not like any woman I've met before, and I'm a stupid man that has never been in a real relationship. I forget and do dumb things. I'm going to make a mistake, but I don't want to lose you, baby."

I grabbed his hand and laced my fingers through his. "How about I tell you when you're out of line? I mean, it'll probably be at the top of my lungs as I'm throwing things, but I promise I'll let you know. Okay?"

He laughed. "That is a deal I will take." He reached up and traced the line of my jaw. "Afterall, It would suck to have fallen in love with you just to end up screwing it all up."

"W-What? You've fallen in love with me?"

His hand paused on my cheek. "Yeah, I have."

"I think I might be falling, too."

"Yeah? You're willing to make this a long-term thing?" Smiling, he rolled closer. "I can think of a very good way to start. I do believe I've caught my breath."

I gasped, playfully swatting him away. "I'm not a toy, you big man, you."

"Oh, yes you are," he said, dragging his hips across my thigh. He was getting harder very quickly. "A very addictive, beautiful, amazing toy that I plan to entertain me for a very long time. I just have to make sure I give you some very good reasons to keep coming back."

I threw my leg over his hip and pushed him onto his back so I was straddling his pelvis. "There's one that comes to mind. In fact, I think I could get used to this."

"I hope so," he whispered, running his hand down my spine. "I plan to make sure this is a night you will never forget."

Chapter 5

Emmy

I woke up to the sound of a phone ringing. I'd been deep asleep and was still groggy as I heard a man ask, "What is it?"

In the quiet of the bedroom it was easy to hear a man's voice respond. "We have an emergency, sir."

"Can it wait?" Max snarled.

"It can't," the voice replied.

"I'll call you right back." He leaned over to me and kissed me deeply on the lips. He broke our embrace and stared into my eyes. "I'll be right back," he said. And before I could respond, Max turned and walked out of the room, leaving me a bit slack-jawed.

Max

"This had better be good, Rex!" I roared as I shut the door to one of the spare bedrooms in the suite. "I was right in the middle of… well, I was doing something."

"I'm afraid we have a situation, sir," Rex said flatly. Rex was my go-to guy, a fixer, the kind of guy you go to when the usual methods just don't work out. I'd had him dig up dirt on my competitors, bribe corrupt city officials or blackmail them when they tried to extort me, and most importantly, get me evidence that my Carmella hadn't been honest with me. "What is it?"

"It's Carmella, sir," he replied. "What's she done now?"

"I just had a call from my guy at the hospital," Rex replied. "They said Carmella was brought in on a suicide attempt and says she won't speak to anyone but you."

"Fucking shit," I growled, rubbing my forehead. This wasn't real. I knew it instantly. Carmella had pulled this kind of shit before whenever she didn't get her way. It was an obvious, desperate attempt to get me to stay with her so she could keep spending my money. Carmella was the definition of crazy. She'd roped me in by acting normal, turned out she was a total sociopath. I should have seen it earlier. "Has the press gotten word yet?"

"Not yet," Rex replied. "My guy recognized her and checked her in under a different name. But I'm not sure how long we can keep it a secret. Someone's going to see her and make a phone call."

"All right, I'll call her," I replied. Shit. Shit. Shit! Everything was going great and then this shit happens? I was definitely wishing I'd never met Carmella to begin with, and worse yet, wishing I'd listened to my mom. I immediately called Pete, Rex's guy at the hospital.

"Hello, sir."

"How is she?" I asked.

"She's fine," he replied. "Obvious attention-seeking maneuver. Didn't even take enough pills to kill a toddler, but she's saying she'll go home and try it again if she doesn't talk to you. Says she'll go to the press."

"Fuck," I growled as heard him walking.

"I guess you blocked her calls?" Pete asked.

"Had to," I replied. "Let me talk to her."

"Hey, sweetie cakes."

"Don't call me that," I growled. "What the fuck is this, Carmella? Another pathetic attempt to win me back?"

"I'll go to the papers!" she hissed. "I'll tell them the distress of you leaving me was too much and that's why I tried to kill myself!"

"You think they'll believe that?" I bluffed.

"Even if they don't, it'll be everywhere," she smiled. "Do you really want that kind of shit out there ruining your nice guy reputation?" Carmella was the kind of girl who'd light herself on fire just to make sure you burned too

"What do you want, Carmella?"

"You," she replied, her voice morphing into sweetness.. "Don't you want to try again, Maxy?"

"Don't call me that."

31

"We were so good together!"

"Yeah, until you tried to ruin me," I growled. "Until I realized just how crazy you are."

"So I made a mistake," she mewled, putting on her best little girl voice. "Don't you think you could try and forgive me?"

"Go to the fucking papers, Carmella," I snapped. "Say whatever you want. I've found someone else now and I'm going to be happy with her. I really don't care what anybody else says!" And with that, I hung up the phone. I was sweating and wanted to break something. Knowing the only thing that could take my mind off Carmella and her insanity was waiting for me back in the bedroom and I had to see her. All I wanted was her.

Chapter 6

Emmy

What could be happening? I thought as I did another lap around the enormous bedroom. The voice had said it was an emergency. Was it family trouble? Something with his business? His parents? Oh, God, I thought. He doesn't have kids I don't know about, does he!?

"Relax, Emmy," I told myself as I leaned back against the table and looked down at my pussy, still dripping with his cum. I was still in a daze from what he'd done to me. My pussy was aching and I was more turned on than I'd ever been in my entire life just thinking about it.

I didn't really know what was going on or how in the hell I'd fallen so hard for Max so quickly, but what I did know was that I wanted him back here. With a sigh, I continbued to walk around the room, not caring if I was naked.

"Hey baby," he said as his arms suddenly wrapped around me. How had I not heard him coming into the room? Feeling my cheeks heating up I realized that I was blushing. Blushing and dripping wet for him. I wanted him to take me, have his way with me again, but I could see that something was bothering him.

"Is something wrong?" I asked.

"No," he shook his head. "My ex- girlfriend, she faked another suicide attempt to try to get me to go back with her."

"Oh…" I replied softly. "So…you're going to…?"

"Hell no!" he snapped. "I'd chew off my leg before I got back with that bitch!"

A sense of relief washed over me, but I could see he was still really upset by what had happened, so I pressed my body against his and stroked his strong chin with my index finger. "It's okay," I told him. "She's not here now. It's just you and me."

"I'm sorry," he growled. "I shouldn't let her get to me. You and I were enjoying a wonderful night, and…"

"That's right," I said as I grabbed him right by his power center. "We were. And now we are again." I pressed my lips against his and opened my mouth to accept his tongue. I could tell he wasn't expecting this from me, and I smiled as he kissed me back.

The drawstring of his sweatpants came undone with a quick tug and I slid my hand inside and found what I was looking for. Wow…I thought. There's just nothing wrong with this man! And that was putting it mildly. His cock wasn't even fully hard yet, but it was thick and heavy in my hand, and as I began stroking it, it continued to rise until it was like a hot rod of steel that I could barely wrap my fingers around. From the sounds Max was making, he seemed to be enjoying what I was doing to him.

I got down on my knees and looked up at Max, feeling more submissive than I'd ever felt before. It felt so good to relinquish control over to a man like Max. In fact, I knew right then that Max was the only man I could ever do this for. I tugged his sweatpants down all the way and his cock sprang out and hung before him like something a Greek god would possess. I licked my lips as I started to salivate and looked up at him.

Max's strong fingers gripped my hair like he was putting it in a ponytail and he pushed my head down. I opened my mouth and accepted his cock, tasted the sweet and salty precum against my tongue and moaned. He began to move my head up and down, showing me how he wanted me to suck it. "That's good," he groaned, filling me with warmth.

My cheeks stretched around his thick head. He was so thick, hard and warm. Being submissive in this way was new to me and not anything I'd ever known I would be into. It had never been anything I'd fantasized about, and I knew that it was only Max who could make me feel this way. Whatever had happened to him with his ex-girlfriend, whatever stress he was feeling at the moment, I was taking that pressure off of him and providing him with something else.

"You're so sexy," he said as he caressed my head. "Let's see how much you can take down your throat?"

I pulled back and licked my lips as I looked up at him and nodded. I grabbed the base of his cock and opened wide. I opened and accepted his girth once more, tasted precum on my tongue and took a deep breath as he pushed the back of my head down. Don't cough, I told myself. Don't gag! I was sure I was going to.

To my complete shock, every single inch of his monstrous dick slid down my throat until my nose was pressing against his sculpted abs and his balls were pressing against my chin. "Ho-ly fuck!" Max growled.

I wanted to cry out in victory, but that was impossible. Instead, I flashed my eyes up at the gorgeous man above me and melted when I saw the look on his face. His face was filled with lust and intent, and I took a deep breath through my nose as he pulled back slightly and began to fuck my throat.

There was nothing for me to do but kneel before him and take it. It was so submissive, but I felt powerful at the same time. He was turned on by me. He wanted me. I wasn't some crazy ex out to ruin him, or some girl just looking for a paycheck; I wanted to please him and he seemed to know that.

His cock flexed in my throat and I felt the warmth of more precum drip down the back of my tongue. I swallowed as his eyes grew more intent. His hand tightened on my head, pulling my hair so tight it almost hurt. And all that did was turn me on even more. "I'm going to come, gorgeous," he growled.

"Mmm!" I moaned. I wanted it so badly.

"Fuck...I'm going to come so hard, baby," he groaned as his eyes rolled back and closed. His cock pulsed and I felt a splash of warm cum spray into my throat with incredible force. I swallowed as fast as I could, not letting a single drop escape. It was the hottest thing I'd ever experienced, and I was right on the edge myself.

He shook and groaned like a giant and then relaxed. I pulled back and gasped, leaving his cock glistening with spit and cum and smiled up at him like the proudest girl in the world. "I did it," I mewled. "I took it all."

"No one's ever done that before," he panted. "You are a goddess."

"Really?" I whispered as he leaned down, took me underneath the arms and lifted me so I was standing before him. I thought he might hold back from kissing me but he didn't. His lips met mine and I pressed my body hungrily against his.

"That felt amazing, gorgeous," he whispered. "But I'm not even close to being done with you."

Chapter 7

Max

"Max?" my sweet Emmy asked, as we watched the sun come up from bed.

"Yes, baby?"

"I'm not on the pill," she replied. "Do… do you want me to like go get Plan B or something?"

"What do you mean?" I protested. "I'm a billionaire. Don't you want to get pregnant and rope me in for millions of dollars?"

"What?!" Emmy stammered, sitting up on the bed, her face suddenly red with anger. "What kind of a thing is that to say?"

I shut her up with a kiss, pulled back and stared deeply into her eyes. "I know, baby. I'm just kidding. I know you're not like that."

Emmy sighed a sigh of relief, "Thank god."

"But to answer your question, no, I don't want you to go get Plan B."

Emmy's eyes went wide. She couldn't believe what she was hearing, but I could see how much it meant to her. I waited. I didn't want to say too much. This was a critical moment for us both and I wanted her to feel it. "You're okay with that?"

"Are you?" I asked her. "Because this isn't just a night of passion for me, Emmy. This is something more. I knew there was something special about you from the minute I saw you cleaning my room. And now I know it for sure."

"Know what…?" she asked hesitantly.

"That I love you, Emmy," I told her. It felt like the most natural thing in the world to say and the sparkle in her eyes when I said it confirmed what I already knew.

"I…I love you too, Max." We kissed again and I could barely stop myself from smiling. She's mine now. I don't know how long we kissed, and I could have kept going for days, but it occurred to me that we might want to clean up, so I sat up and looked down at her gorgeous body. She was glowing like a goddess.

"Why don't we take a shower and get some sleep for a few hours?" I suggested.

Emmy arched her back and extended a hand like I was going to put a ring on it. "The billionaire and the maid getting dirty in the shower?"

"Sounds like a porno," I chuckled.

"Or a romance novel," she countered. I took her hand and led her towards the attached bathroom, but just as I was turning on the water, there was a knock at the door. I groaned. "You've got to be fucking kidding me." I turned to my beautiful Emmy, who was trying her best to hide the disappointment in her face. "I'm sorry, baby. This should just take a second," I said as I kissed her. "Get started and I'll join you."

I couldn't help but worry as I stepped into the shower alone. I'd had the best time with Max and I kept worrying that something was going to go wrong. "Don't think like that, Emmy," I told myself as I reached for the loofah and spread some of Max's body wash over it. I recognized the smell instantly and smiled as I began to wash myself. "It's probably just room service or something." That was it. What else could it be?

What if he's hiding something…? I shook the thought from my mind. What was I doing? I'd just fallen hard for the man of my dreams and let him come inside me and now I was going to doubt him? No, I thought. I'm not going to let myself do that.

Just as I was lathering up, I heard screaming from the room. "Where is she?" a woman's voice shrieked. "I'll fucking kill her!" My heart instantly went into overdrive. There was no doubt in my mind that her meant me, and my fight-or-flight instincts kicked in immediately. Adrenaline coursed through me as I quickly tried to rinse the soap from my body.

I was already on high alert and my anger was right beneath the surface, and there was nothing like standing naked by yourself to make you feel vulnerable. "Is she in here?" the voice screamed as whoever it was stormed into the bedroom. I heard the door slam against the wall and heavy footsteps coming closer.

"She's in the fucking shower, isn't she?!" The door to the shower burst open and I barely had time to snatch a towel from the rack and throw it around my body before a furious-looking woman barged into the room looking like she was ready to kill someone… me.

"There she is!" she shouted, pointing an angry finger at me. I cried out as she lunged at me, but she moved like a ninja and lashed out with a slap before I could get out of the way. Her palm stung my cheek and I froze in shock.

She wound up for a punch and would have landed it had it not been for Max, who leapt out from behind her and grabbed her in his arms. "Carmella!" he roared. "Get away from her!"

"Fuck you!" Carmella shrieked, thrashing out with her elbows. My heart was pounding so hard I thought it might explode.

"Go, Emmy!" Max cried out. "Get out of here!"

"Yeah, whore!" Carmella snarled. "Get your whore ass out of here and leave me and my husband alone!" Max started to respond but was cut off when one of her elbows slammed into his mouth, causing him to stagger back against the sink.

I wasted no time racing out of the room and back into the walk-in closet where I'd left my clothes. Husband!? My heart started to shatter as I scrambled back into my clothes, the shouting growing louder from the other room.

As I stepped out into the hallway, a severe-looking man in a suit passed me walking quickly in their direction. "You need to go," he said as he passed me. That was it. You need to go. Like I was no longer welcome in Max's room.

The world felt like slow motion as I left his hotel suite and ran down the hall. I took the stairs to the first floor and raced out the door into the night. What was I thinking? I thought as I ran over to my car which looked as out of place here as I suddenly felt.

Carmella, despite being hysterical, was gorgeous and definitely model material. She was obviously one of the elite, one of those women who belonged in the Hamptons among the Who's Who crowd and old money. And what was I? Just a broke girl trying to take care of her depressed mother and little brother and sister working as a maid. I'd been swept off her feet by a smooth-talking man who was no doubt practiced in the game he'd just run on me. I bet he even had himself snipped and that's why he didn't care about coming inside me.

"Leave me and my husband alone!" Her words stung like a thousand wasps, but they were nothing compared to Max's that had hit me like a gut shot. "Go, Emmy! Get out of here!" I didn't need to be told twice. I was like a prey animal in flight mode as I climbed into my car, turned the key in the ignition and gunned it out of the parking lot.

Tears began to streak down my eyes as I sped down the road. The beautiful homes in this part of town taunted me as if to reinforce the truth that I was just a girl who didn't belong here. How could Max be so fucking perfect and a liar at the same time? I'd never understood how women managed to get themselves roped into relationships with men who weren't faithful to them, but I guess I'd been duped too. I should have never listened to him.

Chapter 8

Emmy

I stormed into the house like a bull on stampede. If the door had busted off its hinges, I wouldn't have even cared. Mom just about jumped out of her skin as I stormed in. She'd been sleeping on the couch and leapt up with both fists in the air like it was a home invasion. "Emmy! What the hell?"

It didn't even get my attention that she wasn't in her bedroom. I went into the kitchen, grabbed a glass of water and guzzled it. Then I was over at her side and slumping down on the couch wiping tears off my face. "Well, this doesn't look good," she said.

I made a face and started crying again. "He has a wife!" I blabbered. "A wife! And she slapped me!"

"Who does, baby? Who's made you cry?" Mom asked in confused concern.

"Max. The man I was seeing."

"Oh, god, I'm so sorry baby," Mom said as she slid closer to me and wrapped an arm around me. "Tell me everything."

"I stopped by his room at the resort after work because Carolyn said he had forgotten to give me my tip before the weekend. And I-I…" My voice trailed off as I thought back to our time together. "And we did it!" I cried out, slapping my in embarassment.

"Tell me what happened, Emmy. His wife showed up?"

I nodded and groaned again, feeling like I'd volunteered to be a knife-thrower's assistant thinking, naïvely, that I would be fine, but instead ended up with a blade buried in my heart. "There was a knock on the door as I went to the shower to wash up and the next thing I know this crazy woman is screaming at me and trying to kill me."

"Jesus…"

"She slapped me. She called me a whore…"

"You're not a whore, Emmy," she said firmly.

"Yeah, well, I certainly felt like one when she called him her husband," I cried.

"Baby, I'll stay up with you tonight and we'll figure everything out. I'm sorry I've been a terrible mom lately. You've been taking care of us when I should have been taking care of you," Mom said, pulling me closer. "I can't imagine how you're feeling. You just tell me what you want. Pizza? Ice cream?"

I turned and looked out the window as I heard the rain begin to fall, streams of water mirroring the tears running down my cheeks. "I just kind of want to sit here for a while," I admitted.

"Okay, sweetie," Mom smiled. "The kids are over at a friend's house so it's just us tonight. If that psycho bitch even tries to show up here, I'll go Momma Bear on her ass!"

Something approximating a laugh squeezed itself from my lips and as I settled into a more comfortable position on the couch a moment of even greater self-criticism came over me. What was I doing? Running home to Momma? I a survivor! This wasn't going to break me! But as hard as I tried to convince myself that that was true, I just couldn't believe it.

This was the darkest self teaching moment of my life. I don't know how long it was that I lay there on the couch, wrapped in a blanket and curled up in Mom's arms, but eventually I heard my phone buzz and picked it up to see Max calling.

"Is it him?"

"Yes," I replied, ignoring the call. "Fuck him." Stupidly, I threw the phone over my head and heard it hit the wall and clatter to the floor. Mom gasped but didn't say anything. It was probably broken, but so was my heart, and there was no fixing either of them. It buzzed again a few seconds later, chattering across the faded linoleum floor that I hated with all my heart.

Compared to Max's fancy mansion, I was living in squalor. He was up there with his wife, having one of their rich-people-problems fights that they would undoubtedly get over, while I was lying here wondering how we were going to survive the coming months without ending up on the streets. This was just one of those moments you had to stew in and be miserable until it passed, if it passed.

As much as I wanted to hate him, I couldn't and that frustrated me more than anything else. When I pictured him, I still got butterflies. When I thought about the things he'd said to me, how his touch felt, how his lips tasted and his tongue felt on my body, I still melted.

It wasn't fair! How could I still have these feelings for him after what happened to me? He'd lied to me and I'd been assaulted by his freaking wife. I should have been able to cut the cord immediately, but something was holding me back. 'Don't love him, Emmy,' I tried to tell myself, but I would have had better luck telling a lion not to hunt the gazelle. I did love Max, and that's what made what had happened so terrible

I closed my eyes and curled up in my mother's like I was a child who'd just broken their favorite toy, when a firm knock came from the door. I sat up immediately and Mom stood up. She stepped into the kitchen and opened the drawer where we kept the mace and held it at the ready as she approached the door. "Who's there?" she asked.

"Max Harrison!" Max's voice called back. "Is Emmy there? I need to speak to her, please." Mom looked over at me and, when I didn't answer, shouted back at him. "I don't know any Emmy! I suggest you leave before I call the police!"

There was a long pause before he answered that felt like an eternity. I realized my entire body was tense and I was staring at the door like a hopeful child staring at the TV before her favorite movie came on. "Emmy," he spoke, his voice low and firm, loving even. "Please. I know you are there. Let me in, baby. I have to explain what happened back there."

"I told you, there's no Emmy here," Mom started to say again, but I cut her off.

"What is there to explain?" I asked. "You're fucking married, Max!"

"I'm not," he replied. "She's my ex-girlfriend."

"Bullshit!"

"Baby, please," he said. I could hear the sincerity in his voice…couldn't I? "Just open the door so I can look into your eyes."

"Don't do it," Mom whispered.

"I-I have to," I whispered back as I got to my feet.

"He's probably lying," she hissed. She was right; Max could have been lying. But his voice still had me bound to him like ropes of gold circling my body, and I had to look him in the face and hear his explanation. So I got up, walked over to the front door and opened it.

Max stood on my steps, soaking wet and devastatingly gorgeous like something out of the movies. "Hey, gorgeous," he smiled.

"How did you find me?" I asked, unable to contain a little humorous jab. "Get your people to hunt me down or something that a rich person would do?"

"That guy you passed in the hallway, remember?" he asked. "He works at the resort. He spoke to Carolyn."

"Great, now I can't even trust my boss."

"Emmy, I'm so sorry. Carmella Dannings is someone I used to see to take care of my needs. It was never anything more than that."

"She called you her husband and you told me to leave. How am I supposed to think that was anything other than the truth?"

"I didn't want her to hurt you anymore than she already had. Remember the first time I was called out for an emergency? That was because Carmella had checked herself into the hospital threatening to kill herself unless she spoke with me. She wanted me to get back together with her. I have no love in my heart for her at all. She's just a terror in my life now, a nightmare I've been doing my best to manage and failing."

"Sounds believable," Knowing I wasn't in my right mind, I turned back to Mom to get her take. She had her lips twisted up like she was thinking, but she didn't seem obviously put off by his explanation.

"I can show you the restraining order I just had placed on her," Max continued. "But I don't have it with me, but I can have my lawyer fax it to the resort. Or…"

"Or?"

"You and your family can come home with me like we talked about."

"Home, with you?" I asked, shocked by his use of the word. My body shook at his touch and I felt myself starting to calm down. My heart was actually beating like a normal human's again instead of a race horse's.

"That's right," he said, taking my hand. "Our home, Emmy. It's where you belong. The police have Carmella in custody now and I've filed a restraining order against her and started to go into PR defensive mode in case she decides to try to slander my name with lies. I want to put all of this behind me and move on, Emmy. The only way I can do that is with you at my side."

I groaned miserably as the last of my defenses crumbled beneath his suave, genuine, incredible assault. I looked back at Mom who smiled and nodded. My legs went weak and I tumbled forward into Max's arms. I didn't even care that he was soaking wet. In fact, there was something romantic about it and as I pressed my head against his chest and felt his strong hand in my hair, I could also feel his heartbeat against my cheek, strong, steady and firm… just like him.

"You'd better not be lying to me," I whispered as he held me so wonderfully tight.

"I will never lie to you, Emmy," he answered and I believed him.

"Good," I giggled as the greatest feeling of relief and love washed over me like a warm, clear blue wave. "Because I might just have to kill you if you are."

Epilogue

Emmy

Two weeks later

Max was perfect. I mean, literal perfection. From his model good looks, to his athlete's physique, to his pornstar Adonis dick, to his sweet personality and incredible mind that kept him at the top of business, I woke up every morning feeling like the luckiest woman in the world.

He moved my Mom and siblings into the large guesthouse behind us. He got a tutor for Marc and Anna until we figured out what school we wanted them to go to. I was worried that they would be angry about moving but the opposite was true. Max spent time with them every evening and Marc in particular was thriving.

Mom was doing so much better. Max's mom had quickly taken her under her wing and the two of them were like two peas in a pod. I hadn't seen Mom so happy in way too long. I really meant the world to me.

It was for all of those reasons, and so many more, that I was fumbling around the kitchen doing my best to make a decent chicken parmesan for him for when he got home from work. He was closing a big deal today and I wanted to pamper him. Besides, I had something big to tell him.

As I beat the chicken breast with a rolling pin to flatten it, I thought back to all that had happened since we met and how everything had come together after it seemed like my entire life was going to fall apart. Max had showed me all of the paperwork againt Carmella, who must have realized it wasn't smart to go up against us and hadn't made good on any of her threats to slander Max's name in the press.

That had made us both happy, of course, but it was what Max did for me that really had me feeling like I had my feet on the ground again. He set me up to go back to school through remote learning and I was on my way to finally getting my business degree. I wanted to be the best woman I could be with a man like Max by my side.

I was just starting to coat the chicken in the egg wash when I heard the door and turned to see my beautiful man come inside. "Oh, rats! I wanted to have this done by the time you got home," I protested as he came up to me and gave me a kiss on the cheek and a butt squeeze to go along with it.

"What is it?" he asked. "Shrimp scampi?"

"Chicken parmesan," I laughed. "I just got done beating these breasts like they owed me money."

"I know there's some kind of sexual innuendo joke to make here," Max chuckled. "I just can't think of it right now. Here, put that down for a second and wash your hands, would you?"

"But I'm right in the middle of it," I whined. "I wanted to make something nice for you."

"And I appreciate that, and you will, but right now I need you to put that aside and wash your hands for me, okay?" He had a serious look on his face that I knew meant he didn't want me to argue with him, so I nodded and started washing my hands in the sink.

"Did everything at work go all right?" I asked.

"I don't wanna talk about work right now," he told me, taking me by the wrist and leading me from the kitchen. This wasn't like him. He was always a man who liked to be in control, but he was never mysterious, and whatever was going on now was mysterious. I grabbed a dish towel and dried my hands as he led me up the stairs to the second floor and our bedroom. He stopped, turned to face me and smiled.

"Okay, you're being weird," I said softly. "What's going on?"

"Do you remember the day we first met, Emmy?"

"What kind of a question is that?" I laughed. "How could I ever forget?"

"Little did I know that morning that when I came out of the shower my life would forever be changed for the better." His words wrapped around my heart and squeezed until I felt the tears begin to well up in my eyes.

"Awww," I moaned, pouting my lower lip at my beautiful boyfriend as he took my hand in his.

"That night I claimed you and made you mine forever." I couldn't speak. Something inside me wanted to scream with happiness, but I was afraid that if I did anything, I'd ruin the moment and what I thought was about to happen. "And now, Emmy," he smiled. "I want to make it official."

I gasped and clamped a hand over my mouth as Max got down on one knee in front of me, reached into his jacket pocket and pulled out the most unbelievable ring I'd ever seen.

"Emmy Jackson," he said. "Will you make me the happiest, luckiest man in the world and be my wife?"

That was it. Tears streamed from my eyes as I choked back a sob and nodded vigorously. It couldn't be more perfect. I watched, hypnotized as he slid the beautiful ring onto my finger and smiled. I threw myself into his arms and he held me as we rocked back and forth like a couple of high schoolers slow dancing to the last dance of the night.

"You know, baby...," I whispered. "There was another reason I wanted to cook for you tonight."

"Oh, yeah?" he replied.

"Yes," I said, pulling back so I could stare into his eyes. "I'm pregnant."

THE END

About the Author

Euryia Larsen grew up thinking that what she was being told about the world was only part of the story. She loves myths both historical and modern and often sees the the possibility in 'what if'. A good romance with strong 'alpha' heroes and even stronger heroines that can be a partner for them are her favorite kinds of books. If the heroines are just a tad crazy, even better.

Euryia is a stay at home mom of two beautiful daughters, four crazy cats, three crazier dogs and a husband to round out the bunch. She deals with her fair share of issues while dealing with Fibromyalgia and other complications and as a result, she's finds an escape in books where there is always a happily ever after. She's always been creative and has written for herself as an audience for longer than she can remember.

I'd love to hear your thoughts on this or myths or books in general or even just a hello.

Check me out at
http://www.EuryiaLarsen.com
or feel free to email me at
EuryiaLarsenAuthor@gmail.com

Other Books by Euryia Larsen

Broken Butterfly Dreams

Standalone Novellas:

The Mobster's Violet

Clover's Luck

Touch of Gluttony

Halloween Darkness

Another Notch On Her Toolbelt

Sealed With A Kiss

Fate's Surprise

Midnight Rose

His Curvy Housemaid

Hello, Goodbye

The Dark Side (Dragon Skulls MC):

Saint

Beautiful Smile

Twisted Savior

Belladonna Club:

To Trap A Kiss

His Peridot

Not the Good Guy (Kazon Brothers)

with Kyra Nyx:

Kazon Brothers Box Set

The Dark

The Beast

The Villain

Saga of The Realms:

Power of Love – Prequel Novella (Paperback)

Power of Love – Prequel Novella (Free Ebook)

Bonded By Destiny

War of Giants

Printed in Great Britain
by Amazon